The Water Statues

Fleur Jaeggy

The Water Statues

Translated from the Italian
by Gini Alhadeff

A NEW DIRECTIONS
PAPERBOOK ORIGINAL

© 1980 Adelphi Edizioni S.P.A., Milan
Translation © 2021 by Gini Alhadeff

Published by arrangement with Adelphi Edizioni, Milan.

First published as a New Directions Paperbook Original (NDP1508) in 2021
Manufactured in the United States of America
Design by Erik Rieselbach

Library of Congress Cataloging-in-Publication Data
Names: Jaeggy, Fleur, author. | Alhadeff, Gini, translator.
Title: The water statues / Fleur Jaeggy ; translated from the Italian by Gini Alhadeff.
Other titles: Statue d'acqua. English
Description: First edition. | New York, NY : New Directions Publishing Corporation, 2021.
Identifiers: LCCN 2021021184 | ISBN 9780811229753 (paperback) | ISBN 9780811229760 (ebook)
Subjects: LCGFT: Novels.
Classification: LCC PQ4870.A4 S7313 2021 | DDC 853/.914—dc23
LC record available at https://lccn.loc.gov/2021021184

10 9 8 7 6 5 4 3 2 1

New Directions Books are published for James Laughlin
by New Directions Publishing Corporation
80 Eighth Avenue, New York 10011

The Water Statues

for Ingeborg

DRAMATIS PERSONÆ

BEEKLAM
VICTOR, *Beeklam's servant*
REGINALD, *Beeklam's father*
LAMPE, *Reginald's servant*
THELMA, *Reginald's wife*
ROSALIND

THELMA'S FRIENDS
MAGDALENA
KASPAR
KATRIN

I

Though the years vanish as swiftly as ever, sorrow, and life coming to an end make time seem too long. I spend entire days observing nature, the gradual calming of nature: at such times my ideas become vague, undecided; without tiring them, a wild sadness rests in my eyes, and my gaze wanders over the rocks all around; every place here is a friend I am happy to see again. And somehow places I am not familiar with become my property; there is one spot there, high up on the cliff, from which the limestone humps descend ceremoniously and lethargically down to the water; and it's as though a faint recollection were telling me that I'd lived there — or in the water long ago — though the exact trace of that time has been erased in me.

I was born, said Beeklam, in a house on a hill of boulders. Then he fell silent.

* * *

Ataraxic at the sight of the boulders, I opened the window to something very "fine" and welcome reaching me from the cracks between the rocks — an echo, repeating the last two or three syllables of a sentence, or by omitting one letter, resounding like a reply or a warning, perhaps even a hiss. Or a condemnation. *Shh shh shh*, said my father, interrupting in a low stinting voice, announcing the death of his wife (and my mother) Thelma. Who hasn't seen children laugh while adults cry? Though, so as not to disturb him, I was laughing almost soundlessly, almost ruefully. Much has been said of the crystalline, celestial, happy laugh of children. I had often noticed the laughter of children, of the few I'd had a chance to meet: those few would laugh about everything—at themselves, at cool and collected dromedaries, at the boats of the Yucatan, at iridescent fish scales, and so on, ad infinitum: at their mothers, at the ample arms that held them, at the mighty arms that held me, too, when they came to our house as though in lifeboats to convey their solidarity with our mourning and silence. Those arms clasped me to them, hot gusts frosted my ears. In a detached tone of voice, as though surprised by the many visitors, I discussed the matters of the day. Mournful backs rested against our ample armchairs, and the blend of voices seemed to me melodious.

Approaching from one side the seated people, I became aware of something multicolored—words pronounced distinctly, an attitude unaccustomed to ceremony, the slow movements of girdled bodies—I was even caught unawares by a nuanced red cherry resting on a hat (and that Ceres basket on the head was filled with other meaty berries as time sped by all too quickly).

Fragments of shadow announced day's end.

"Ladies," I said, rising on my stilts, "thank you, and good-bye."

I continued to wave goodbye even from the staircase.

They bent the flesh of their pale faces, Chinese porcelain

cups in hand, and fingers waved back automatically, swiftly, rustling, remote. I climbed up to my room to greet the decline of light, perhaps so as not to forget the exact descent of night that day, that social day of the loss of my mother.

Like an island rising out of the mud, some joie de vivre spread its glow around the empty chair's silent tyranny. The chair in which Thelma (just like the spiders that silently spin) used to weave was wrapped in a tight-fitting slipcover.

* * *

BEEKLAM: I saw the widower, long and narrow, as though in flight, sit, patiently undoing the petit point on its stretcher, that lovely harmony of a mountain landscape swept away by the man's reckless fingers; such was his skill (as though he'd done little else in life) and zeal in untangling the colored threads that soon that perforated skein displayed its natural tint—of soggy snow.

* * *

Following a blind alley in Amsterdam, not far from the harbor, one reaches a dark stone building almost unwittingly. Metal screens clatter on the windows. The front gate is always open. White porcelain tiles cover the floor of the entrance; propped up by the mighty, almost black stone arms of two broken sirens, its vault holds the open eye of a window. Stumps of other arms are scattered across the ceiling. Little remains of the pink flesh color, some of the cobalt blue, and a few gold stars. It was once a sky. This is where Beeklam lived.

BEEKLAM: Shut the doors.

VICTOR: They are double doors and they are shut.

BEEKLAM: So what's that light filtering in endlessly?

VICTOR: There are cracks.

BEEKLAM: Well, block them off.

"The cracks," Beeklam repeated, raising his head by about three finger widths, "or untimely passersby. Yesterday they were down by the wall, standing stiff, with black sashes at their waists and a positive look in their eyes. Were they meditating? Our orbs clashed. I'd lowered my gaze heavily. When I opened my eyes again, I saw them crouching over the magnolias. I went up to the window: they had pointed beards that stood out against white ruff collars."

"Thank you," I said in a falsetto, clearing my throat, and on tiptoe: "Call me a thief, a thief of ceremonies." My words were met by a rustling of fibers.

Sometimes one meets people who look distracted, they don't seem to care about anything; they don't look at people passing by, not at the men or at the women; they walk along in a dream, their pockets empty, their gaze empty of thought, yet they are the most passionate people on earth: collectors. Beeklam was one of them. He lived in the basement of his large house which was filled with statues, most of them commemorative effigies—a lapidary presence stretching practically all the way down to the sea. Because his basement, like the sewers, went down to the water. It was a relief to Beeklam to know that any gap or crack would give a sense of the movement of waves: of a submerged world he believed to be populated by other statues with feet (if they still had them) tied to stones; and whose knuckles of stone knocked on his walls. No one shooed him away when he rested his head on the wall and waited—perhaps for the statues of water to return, or to summon him. The child now wished to live as though he'd drowned. But he heard rising up from the sewers the rustling sleep of serpents. No one shooed him away because he was quite alone.

He'd abandoned his newly widowed father to go and "buy statues," he said, and it was as if he were joking. From early childhood, he'd been drawn to figurative imitations of grief and stillness; from childhood he'd been a collector, museums were in him; statues were his playthings, a privilege of all who are born lost and start out from where they end. The child looked at them: he inspected eyelids and napes, drawn into their definitive dimensions of seriousness, some molded by artists of renown, others by unknown workshops. He had a name for each: Rosalind, Diane, Magdalena, Thelma, Gertrud. Those statues with their often amiable faces disclosed the things that dwell in things themselves, vitreous things.

He thought of his father, Reginald, again: of his father's clothes, his obsession with the cold, his seemingly absent, unfocused eyes, and of the term "passed" which he pronounced serenely. "She simply passed before us," Reginald would say of his wife.

But one day the solitary child, his hair ash-colored, ran out of the basement, and stopped before a garden: the sun was going down and drawing a leaden oval mirror over the trees; it seemed to him that the death rattle of eternity resounded between sundown and the night; for the first time he felt buoyed, for the first time he felt as though something was lasting too long—the solar ring had not yet vanished. It's so easy to admire it, it's the last fantasy nature indulges in, it's all color, on fire. Yes, the sun is disintegrating, a squalid pretender to the glory of that Void denied to any who might mention its name or cling to it. It was as though it were saying, "True life is beyond words." Beeklam was surprised to be talking about the sun. A gentleman, meanwhile, whom Beeklam had not failed to spot, all dressed in dark clothes with a white band at the neck, was walking in the garden, as though, after having named every single tree, he'd just let go of Emily Brontë's arm. And now he was tired. He sits on a bench. The geometric flower beds, in the dusk, are dull, the weeds are limp, and a single flower stoops with heroic élan. At that instant the person sitting looks at his watch—and gets up. That man is certainly not interested in company, Beeklam thought: company is tiring, unlike flowers that punctually put an end to the day. And yet, what could have been holding Beeklam back if not a need for company, and for quiet, but that person seems in every way bent on fleeing the only other person present; he has now approached the gate and pulls it shut, snapping its iron padlock. At that moment Beeklam, for no reason on earth, felt he had found a friend; and maybe—he told himself—it would be forever.

"When I was a gardener at the botanical gardens," Victor recounts, "I went in search of memories among the plants: soon it will snow, I thought—and my shovel was already covered in snow. But soon, too, I came out of winter. I locked the gate with the padlock. It's closed, I told a passerby. Imitating a middle-aged man, a boy dressed in dark clothes, with a flower in his buttonhole and a pencil in his breast pocket, asked me simply if I wanted to be his servant. And here, at the botanical gardens, I asked, is where you come looking for servants? The boy half grimaced, then without moving his lips said, 'Your ears, sir. The immense contours of your ears, lit by the lamppost, caught my attention. High and slanted, slowly they went from shadow to lacy light, and from light to shadow; I waited to see who bore that head—the head that wasn't there. You should know that at all times I live among my statues, and by now all that's left for me to look for in the course of my excursions through time is the head of my look-alike.'"

BEEKLAM: In my basements humidity flows everywhere—
it's almost as though the irrigated statues were walking about
aimlessly, like wading birds, sinking toward darkness, falling
below the horizon; but that's just an effect of the watery light,
and of my impatience perhaps. I've found it hard sometimes
to turn my back on the natural call of the waves, and I don't
envy the temperament of vultures or of stars. The blinds at my
windows have been fluttering for fifty years. My city is Amsterdam, where water flows without a true end in sight, and I've
had bloody judicial disputes to do with water, but I won't stray
here onto legal grounds.

BEEKLAM: I've spent a great deal of time in these basements, not that I was weary of the sun, of the open air: I was simply losing control of the hours and of life, so to speak; I was renouncing the rigid definitions of daily life that allow one to succumb to natural heat or to simply depend on the sun and the elements; I was lying down or standing up, or just leaning against a wall in those dank rooms, the dormitories in which my merchandise wandered about briskly, their gaze directed upward, at the bars. Amidst shovels, trophies, discarded shards of marble, my clay guests weave spools of sleep as fine as Malines lace — they sail over the walls, bouncing up like rubber on the dusty steps, rising high toward the light — though they rise in vain, arriving at nothing, not even at beatitude or the depletion of despair. And, as in fairy tales, I went back up, laden with the years.

BEEKLAM: Far away, and beyond my actual dwelling, floated a great wooden carcass—a ship, its sails unfurled—that looked like a dark giant wrapped in a voluminous crimson cape. Could it be the Flying Dutchman, answering the call of our professional mourners? That sinuous crimson color lured me out of the house. I, too, needed to take a walk. It was late spring, the nightingales gayly warbled their long-repressed ecstasies. I was so happy I inadvertently caught my own reflection in a polished wall, polished by fine weather, my eye smiled in the spring light, and that light was reflected in a passerby's smiling pupil. Together we took the same road, and together we sat on a bench by the harbor. Who had chosen that bench? Him or me? I was already vexed that he wore gold earrings. The crushed debris of this harbor in the springtime has the most agreeable resemblance to toys; I never tire of looking at the buckets on the cranes, and at all that heavy matter turning into light loads running along on wires. A scent of celery settled over me. Here in Amsterdam the way fish is displayed is so considerate, but the garlic isn't very white.

I was thinking I should get up from the bench and leave that boy. I had, for the past quarter of an hour, been subjected, and not for the first time—the previous one had lasted almost fifty years—to some interruptions. The boy's smile hadn't yet left his face, and another light shone on it now, who knows why the face had already changed. That sequence of expressions took on an aggressive tinge: I had become too accustomed to all that is durable, absent; to the visual traits of marble and stone figures; and the life, or incarnation of life, in the past quarter of an hour, seemed to commemorate that interval, the empty space that hangs capriciously, like a rope endowed with reason, between two, not altogether convinced, people.

The boy gazed into the distance, more so than necessary, to where the boats floated, beneath a shadow.

I took advantage of his distraction to speak to him softly, so that he could barely hear me: "You know," I said, "my friend will come to get me soon, his name is Victor, and he likes frogs. He was surprised that one could buy such beautiful creatures, beings that bend their head back as we do, displaying the underside of their chin, and the throat; so vulnerable, almost a first fruit of decomposition. With Victor I believe I experience something of the sentiments of owning a slave (I am referring, as you well know, to that age-old, pre-Alexandrian, feeling). That man belongs to me: we play together, I am happy to be in his company, though he's sometimes in the habit of making shrewd remarks. And I'm inclined to believe that one of the most profound relationships possible lies hidden here: I am his slave as he is mine. You might agree with me that in helping another, a friend, there is a vague homicidal passion that's hard to corral into a less murderous sentiment, but I am a little tired today after yesterday's celebrations. (Victor had dared to recall the distant day of our first encounter—such outpourings are always rather exhausting.) Communal life ends up draining the innocence that people who live alone possess. Take you: one can see right away that you live by yourself, that you have no parents; an orphan, I thought, always possesses what we might call a theological ability to live alone, an infallible instinct for classifying people as boring. That, you must know, is something I noticed about you right away. You saw in me a boring person, and I saw that you would rather—and I honestly can't blame you—look at all the insignificant things moving around you, here at the harbor: the cranes, the bruisers bearing crates, the officers' uniforms ... as though your solitude, and the fact of being an orphan, forced you, against your will perhaps, to formulate particularly accurate observations."

The pleasure of still finding himself next to the boy was gone and he felt, even as he spoke, as if that pleasure had been a small trace, left years earlier, of himself. When he saw the boy finally walk away, that was something to be recalled with pleasure, and as a dedicated spectator he watched the sailors go by, slow and bilious.

VICTOR: We walked slowly home, bid farewell to the harbor, to the spring that was ending, to the gullets of the wooden seagulls on the railings, to the aircraft carrier whose metallic effulgence attracted more than one eye.

Next to the canal Beeklam stopped contemplating the trash disturbing the surface of the water and the minuscule ash-colored fish: those brief walks seemed to him his last, and the list of final things seemed brighter to him, more distinct, like something sinking to the bottom.

It started to rain, and the rain never stopped in the days that followed. Beeklam walked skirting the walls, everything was in motion, the reflections of trees trembled on the canals; only a Buddha he caught a glimpse of through a window sat still through that tempest of the elements.

He recognized it, he had given that Buddha to X even before he'd gone to live in the basements. Some faces, in a crowd of child flaneurs, can be unsettling, and they remain suspended there a long time. Then little by little they fade, as though erased by a limp flannel hand. X had been an athlete and an eccentric before putting on weight. He'd grown fat around the age of fifteen, but they'd been done with one another just in time.

He walked on, saw more decorated rooms, people sitting reading the newspaper; the windows of houses proved to him how very quiet the lives of others could be, how pleasant it is to be in an armchair and to hear the patter of rain on glass panes. He was once again persuaded that his life was passing, had passed, and this made him rejoice while admiring the efforts of his fellow creatures, of the Dutch population with their firmness regarding the radiant pinnacles of domestic comfort—such home-sweet-home settings made his heart sink, so much happiness he was happier living without.

Behind another window he saw a woman dressed in black, a widow perhaps, he thought, with a yellowing streak in her hair and cheeks reddened by the heat of a lit fireplace. Her hair hung straight down her mournful back; her hips widened then withdrew into the shoes. A chubby cat dozed, and the embers seemed weary of burning. Maybe the husband and the servant had left, for a better life, and the woman had stopped fighting with the tailor over her last dress. And last things had come up again for the man strolling in the rain: he imagined the woman's husband, a placid gentleman who in the face of chaos shrugs and trustingly goes on playing with the little fireplace spade at the hearth. Though yearning for peace and quiet, he was tempted to ring the bell, he wouldn't have minded sitting next to that lady. But he walked on. The light in the windows was being switched off.

The people were sleeping; the headboards were lasting out the night. Beeklam watched carefully to see if some unholy light might anywhere reveal the face of an acquaintance. They all seemed asleep. A fan-shaped beard emerged from behind a door and disappeared into the night. But Beeklam distributed greetings, kissing the tips of his fingers, as he waited for a signal from handkerchiefs, rags, patches, curtains, anything that might inflate in the wind, in the thrill of spring, and express an aerial jubilation, at least. Where was the spirit of the world hiding its stock of dreamers that night?

It was still raining and his shoes waded through puddles. He stopped in front of a manhole. Beeklam thought of ladybugs, crickets, and jets of water as rivals. He thought of the ending of one book: "Water is a burnt body," and he whispered the line to himself. Someone spoke to him then:

"I read that, too, somewhere, sir. It is always a good thing when along with one's profession—I am a traveling salesman—one has a passion for something one is well acquainted with, such as the sentence you quoted: it gives a sense of the world's luxury. And that two vagabonds appear to leave a library and find one another, that's a luxury, too—their backs turned to each other, at this hour of the night, in that lull before each new oscillation of the pendulum. And yes, dear sir, one can consider this hour, on the whole, to be malignant. An unknown character in antiquity, the traveling salesman: he sees nothing in depth, neither the clients nor the places; he has a good memory for names, and as for things, he appreciates their surface. That's me, sir. It is a luxury, I was saying before I went astray, this nocturnal meeting of ours, that the two of us, without knowing one another, were joined—what a dreadful verb—in our thinking, since, the fatal force of an encounter can manifest itself after all even in hatred."

* * *

BEEKLAM: Then he turned his very tranquil gaze in my direction. And I left.

BEEKLAM: As far as I can remember, Reginald was a tall man, thin and bald, his once rosy complexion had become white as driven snow. Even at the time, I had taken note of his appearance, and I do not intend to make him out to be more handsome than he was. But I had a feeling I'd never see him again.

BEEKLAM: *Late again,* my father used to say, *didn't you hear the gong?*

I was in the garden, I'd answer.

REGINALD (taking a seat at the table): Last spring the asparagus was truly excellent—you are too keen on horticulture, last spring the vegetable garden was more lush, you've abused it.

* * *

The shadow of a long index finger, thin as the sound of a music box, appeared on the wall.

* * *

BEEKLAM: Yes, Daddy, I may have exaggerated.

REGINALD: Doesn't your head spin when you descend into the vegetable garden?

BEEKLAM: Yes, I am conflicted, when I bend down toward the earth, I feel my fingers burning.

* * *

With bleak gravity I contemplate my fingers, curled and folded on the table.

REGINALD: If you are finished we can get up now.

    BEEKLAM: Certainly. I've had nothing to eat, it's healthier not to eat.

* * *

I was shrinking from my bones, and to keep fasters company, Lampe would go by, perfectly erect, his elbows close to his torso. With fierce willpower he sat at the table, as though to prove that the dinner was meant for him alone and that he'd as soon share it with anyone as he would his dreams.

BEEKLAM: Sometimes, in the evening, we'd sit quietly by the fireplace to think, looking at the embers. "It's damp," my father would say at last, and bidding me good night hurried away. We talked a great deal in those years, but I am certain that Reginald's heart never responded with sincere or spontaneous ardor to the words that gushed from his son's youthful throat. I had in me a mental stampede of conversations with different people—construction workers, priests, maids, and many others, I was careful to polish my words and breathe life into them, and more often than not the words were beyond the range of my father's precise arguments. Yet father and son kept each other company well; they seldom spoke of what was between them, so distant and fragrant, of the wife and mother, who had "simply passed before us through the door that leads into that world of light where all is radiant, and where one day we'll be reunited in a bond of ineffable beatitude still beyond our grasp." My father Reginald enjoyed speaking like this.

He didn't mind the wait but spared himself, nurturing his health with the little ancillary graces of a jailer, and, when he gently led me by the hand for long salutary walks, it seemed to me that his constant labor on earthly ministrations was nothing but a devout homage to life. He was solicitous of it, and, if a lazy tear nestled in the corner of an eye, he did not brush it away

but remained so, his eye glistening, ardent, in a darkened room,
until a pale light lit his face, so frequently radiant.

For hundreds of evenings the lamp lit those two up as they sat at the same table; Reginald frowning and absentminded, his face bright; Beeklam with a latent light within him, which in that company was always obscured and veiled. There might not have been two men more radically alien to one another. The father, with great composure, either spoke of what interested him, or simply kept quiet. The son racked his brains to find a subject that wouldn't be dangerous, that would spare Reginald fresh proof of his innate cruelty and of his innocent, clueless inhumanity; and Beeklam gingerly traveled the paths of conversation, like a lady who walks along a muddy path holding up her skirts. "Pity the man who does not know mirth," Reginald would say at the end of one of those evenings. "But now," Beeklam would reply, "I must go back to my shovel." And he would go back to the garden. On a bench a toad kept him company: "A slaughterhouse aesthetic must exist."

Lampe descended from an ancient family of the Bernese Oberland. On his little finger he wore a gold ring engraved with a hatchet and a pitchfork. He bore no trace of his warring Protestant ancestors, and from a great aunt he'd inherited the somewhat feminine appearance of his neck and hands. Beneath white skin, blue veins surfaced like rivulets reminiscent of the quiet delicate work of fishermen when they reanimate worms with a bit of water and finally place them in soft sand, in pretty boxes, like little beds or tin coffins, deployed one next to the other, where they might die in peace without relinquishing their freshness right away. They certainly weren't the hands of a laborer. His ancestors had been laborers. When Lampe knocked on Reginald's door, looking for work, he looked like a gentleman offering his services in exchange for loyalty, he offered himself up in a detached way, almost as though in return for a marriage. And like a warrior he had scoured other households, inspecting their owners and the furnishings, he had examined them, and had gone on his way, detached as ever, and more and more wistful. He was not looking for a female employer but for single men, or widowers, and not young. He was looking for a solitude not too unlike his own. There are tasks in domesticity that appear to belong to the world of dreams rather than the crass reality of domestic labor. He was not like his ancestors who descended from the Alps in a fury, raring for action.

On his face had been spread as though with a spatula, an expression of peace, a sermon painted over a pale complexion. Though thin, in the fortress of his bones there was steel.

* * *

Those nimble bones were held up by the certainty that one can float very well without hope; he was indulgent and benevolent to others, and fixed them with a cheerful grim smile. He pecked at adversities here and there as though in life there were but two possible inclinations: toward desire or toward magic, and moreover, as if one were a whitewash for the other.

* * *

Lampe felt at ease, as soon as he crossed the threshold and shook Reginald's hand. Swift, spare, absentminded, the two men had hardly met but were in perfect agreement, two finicky little plants, intimately delighted to have survived a pruning.

LAMPE: Who was the widower? Someone long-limbed. Reginald gave the impression that by his calm devoid of sweetness he had bypassed every disorder. His eyes, he told me, had long looked at the things of this world as though they beheld the Law, to which he felt bound as by a team spirit. And those eyes had also rested on childhood friends with brotherly feelings—Rosalind, Magdalena, and Thelma. Tall, mild, stern in their ways, placid, they offered some of the greatest advantages in life to a man who did not hold much store by the insolent demands of passions. "I am sure you know," he'd say, "the wild sadness that comes when one recalls a happy time." "It is sad to say, dear Reginald," I'd reply, "but I cannot recall a single sentence or gesture of that time, though I can perfectly recall the appearance of some passerby I never met." He thought that was quite enough. Answering him was already an atonement. An atonement could not disturb him. He had known Magdalena, Rosalind, and Thelma forever, they had grown up beside him, they had been loyal as children and remained so. In their brave bonnets they kept all the qualities that come down in a plumb line from a single source: sincerity. Growing up with them, that trait exalted them and brought them to unreasonable solitude. How could such an inner heritage go unnoticed, and why did such rectitude make for a void around them? Only one little boy looked at them, a boy with a sense of justice as finely weighted as a goldsmith's scale. He resigned himself to their company, which made up for his mortification, and he started being a person who was complacent toward anything that might drive him far from life.

REGINALD: I was at ease around Thelma, everything was so sparing, natural, and choleric. Even simplicity seemed painted through the rooms, and, searching for comfort and company, I found something altogether fatal there: the walls paneled in limpid obsequious wood gave off in the fire's warmth a fragrance reminiscent of hot summer hours in swamps. It was as though everything in the rooms and in the house had been mowed; a whiff of puritanical fury had settled on all inanimate things. And so I lifted the wings of my frock coat at the faint, nearly imperceptible shifts in the wood's grain revealing disconsolate elegances — heads, triangular hoods, a delicate skull — as Thelma suggested, "Those are the thoughts of the woodcutter."

* * *

In that temporary calm, Reginald got up in a certain contemplative stupor — and, like a couple of woodcutters, they shook hands. A while later, a brief ceremony joined their two existences. As though they might see better things over there, Thelma's eyes stared into the far distance, cold and calm.

BEEKLAM: Sometimes I wanted to speak to Lampe. I would ask him for news of Reginald, of the house I had lived in, which seemed now to belong only to him, Lampe. As with certain spirits that one doesn't fail to listen to, I could hear his words though he hardly had any voice left—the raucous notes of a crow. But he had much strength. He had walled up the windows.

"Woe to him who has no home," and as he said so, he was absorbed in counting the windows of the house opposite him.

One window had broken panes, held in place by caulking, which drew two profiles of women: the noses touched, the mouths, as though arrested in an exclamation, were almost open. "But there is some pink around the palate," Beeklam said, "and those talking shards invite me to enter; so, after crossing the court-yard, I go up the stairs, the eloquent and austere architecture watching me. A place for tutors, I told myself, and was nearly frightened. I entered into a kind of parlor where I was expected. I was not wrong, the glass faces began to speak: 'It is with great pleasure,' Magdalena said, 'that I shake Lampe's hand, a bony hand issuing from a starched cuff. He walks slowly, as though he has lead in his shoes.' With sensitive fingers she counted the flowers I'd brought. Rosalind was embroidering. Her smooth convex forehead lifted. We agreed that it was a lovely day. They asked me if I'd ever read Anna Katharina Emmerich. No, never, I replied. I stayed a while longer with them, I don't know how long."

Beeklam found himself once again out in the street. The city seemed to him vague and distant, there was a smell of damp flowers; two little girls were fighting, one using her fists, the other a small red umbrella. He admired the elegant confidence of brutality; the feral turn of horror. He continued to watch them like a beggar, and with all his civility. Then he went back to his basements. The statues fainted in the folds of darkness, emitting a brief hum. A wave came between Beeklam and the night. A few millponds remained in cracks in the walls. He found himself listening to the wind as it blew around the building he was about to leave and with his eyes bid farewell to all things.

A thin old woman appeared in the basements, looking around, and smiling over nothing. Perhaps she hoped to find something she might steal. But she only met the gaze of Beeklam, in a dark suit with white stripes, at the far end of an immense room.

* * *

BEEKLAM: A little boy used to live here, he said he wanted to live as someone who'd drowned, and he started collecting statues. The children—you, madam, must be acquainted with some—often say that they want to go back to another world, one they've known, full of incredible paradigms of perfection. The boy remembered well the beauty he hadn't been able to hold on to, more than once he'd said that he wanted to go back there. He had a horror of anything hereditary, because whatever comes to us by natural inheritance belongs to the dead. I am an old gentleman. I listen to children. I have packed up the statues, I was paid well, and now regret not being able to spend that money. I've become rich. I sold three of them on the sly, the best ones: they were called Magdalena, Rosalind, and Thelma. I can't resist betraying anyone giving me orders—or betraying, simply. That child, who was my master, said to me: "Drown them, throw them all in the water, or you'll be cursed. The Flying Dutchman will wring your neck." I don't believe

in anything, I believe only that it's a good thing to betray, I believe that it's a good thing to transgress some part of orders, not
necessarily anything that might bring one well-being, something on the contrary that might bring unhappiness, despair
to others. I have not kept my word, and what is my word, I
have no word, even though I chatter like a phantom. Now she
stares at me without saying a word. Or is about to announce
my death — there must be something calling itself destiny. We
should get along, *ma belle*. I betray, and she takes.

BEEKLAM: Today I went back to the basements, one last time; permit me one more story, the rest is gone: I mean, my statues. Victor sat by the fire. Even a tiger would have rubbed itself against the crinoline of those flames, attracted by the breeze playing through the embers. Winter was about to end and the flames had sunk almost to the ground; ashes fluttered in the darkness. One last flame fell and a whiff of frosty air pushed the door open slowly, as though with one hand, disclosing a detestable crystal-clear dawn.

II

Toward the end of the eighteenth century a phlegmatic giant, with hands that were too small, built a pavilion in a bamboo grove, a hardheaded and ingenious mixture of Eastern and Alpine Swiss ideas, inspired by an obsessive pastoral poise. He was surrounded by a veranda on which the placid talons of leaves spread shade, depth, and disorder. You couldn't see the sea from up there, one only heard the sound of water when it foamed and raged. So, too, leaves ruffled by storms bend as though they were ears. In the fall they would creak and snap. The breeze played with the dust.

In the summer, the landscape was bright, even cheerful; but from September to March, at sunset, with strong winds and gurgling waves washing along the mossy floor, the place conjured only dead sailors and shipwrecks. In the remaining three months, pale ruins of greenery, clay, and frayed flowers live out a life of strife, after shouted invocations to spring. To shout is perhaps excessive, though there was no way to be reborn other than by swearing. "I want you to take this place elsewhere," Katrin said.

When Katrin entered the pavilion for the first time, dust and insects had elegantly coated all the rooms, a rocking chair upholstered in mold and brocade still swayed. The ants, eunuchs of order, proceeded along their teeming avenues on the floor, and a large fly droned loudly on rotten wooden planks.

The little girl's face was set in a strange cramped smile that froze her expression. Cunning and strong as a dervish, her features spelled lust, pride, and greed, which lessened only with the years, as though retreating to avoid being stoned to death. And so the girl seemed to be fighting for her life. Kaspar studied that fuming creature, and to calm himself stroked his hair, which was combed with a side part as if drawn in white chalk.

"There's no need for you to call me Father," said Kaspar. "My eyes never smiled over your crib, if you ever had one. I heard two old women speak of you. They called you Katharina, in memory of a saint they were devoted to."

"You see, Kaspar, those two old women were my only friends, they invited me often, though they never paid attention to me; as I ate, I sat to one side quietly, like a stopped watch. When I entered the house, Rosalind put her book on the table and Magdalena shifted her gaze from her thoughts of the void. I sat next to a tray that had been laid out for me, and imagined I was helping myself with silver serving utensils, linked by a chain. I listened to their colorless and unnatural talk of spirits, meticulously poised between homicide and hysteria; never daring to interrupt them, I helped myself to one or two more browned marzipan potatoes. I knew, as I left, that the voices would fall silent right away and then maybe, touched by that tainted cheer, only the pages of the Bible would rustle."

After a few months the two loners, the girl and Kaspar, became friends to a degree; reticent in speech, they tolerated brief and stinting evening conversations. From hedgerow to ditch, they sometimes ventured to confide in one another; almost apologizing, Kaspar said that he was someone who lived entirely in dreams or on walks — the mere lackey of a pirate ship advancing with its lights dimmed. Katrin mentioned the stern fenced-in buildings only for children that she had noticed more than once; she felt she must have passed through one of them herself; she liked looking at the rows of children removed from Order. In these buildings, any constraint was seen as the enemy, of course, but she had also learned to love the pleasures of hate; her joys were few, and after the strain of gaiety, even the pleasure of hating oneself was not the most uncommon of recreations, for lack of anything better.

In the late afternoon the Order guards drink tea, or port, their faces hovering over the cups like a chorus of withered cherubs; the old cook with pointed ears embroiders and the young school mistresses, for a break from the dismal monotony, all dressed in brown, play cards; perhaps they can still kill time educating, though they hardly ever smile, and at the corners of their lips is an instinctive, measured revulsion. During their hours of rest they never look very animated; they remain seated, staring at the cards, like sentinels who have long since been abandoned at their post by the "real sergeant"—as death was called in there. Now they are making dinner, the bread in a metal basket and butter (not too much of it) on a tin plate. Yet Katrin felt tied to those unembittered beings, and their bent afflictions, living in a sort of penance, in that free zone of humanity, desireless; their foreheads dull, they cough respectfully behind one hand and observe all things in general with a profound air of distraction.

KATRIN: Friday at eleven, during lunch, I became painfully aware, more than ever, of life's crudeness and negligence; a smell of tepid fried food filled the dining hall; through wet soles a draft of cold air gripped one's feet; the walls exuded dampness, and through the windowpanes a fine drizzle could be seen falling from a gray sky. We were sitting at thick black marble tables. An irritating sound of forks and knives cloaked the porridge in martial bleakness. One girl, meanwhile, seated in the middle of the hall, was reading, as usual, an excerpt from a book. I stared at my plate, on the bottom of which something resembling rotten wood seemed to have settled; a domestic proffered a large tray of stewed prunes and rhubarb, the juices lapping against his thumbs. Everything was disgusting. The reader's voice reached my ears in fragments, amid the clatter of cutlery. I heard the name Cleopatra, and shards of sentences: *The keel of her ship shimmered in gold, the sails were crimson ... she sinks her foot in the glaucous wave, on which a pure green ray trembles ... on the vast lagoon are yawning mouths of candid foam ... the flabella were wilting ... Do you have the gracious serpent of the Nile here, the one that kills unobtrusively?*

And so a vision sprang from the filthy plate up to my eyes. I felt the blood beating at my temples, and I may not have managed to disguise the void into which I had fallen. The headmistress, a woman easily given to verdicts of absolution or punishment, realized that I was gripped by some inscrutable witchcraft and her small nervous mouth angrily pronounced my sentence: I had not risen at the signal.

But I had seen the serpent.

One day Kaspar was sitting on a stone bench in the botanical gardens. The trees were very close to him and to his thoughts, which were whispering something regarding his fifty years of silence and seclusion. He pondered some obscure matters he felt attracted to, relating to swamps, soaked reeds, to certain animals' fondness for death, to an officer of the United States Navy. The latter had found, on the Antarctic glaciers, at approximately three thousand feet above sea level, skeletons of seals that had painstakingly dragged themselves up there to die in peace. In old age they don't allow themselves to be molested by creatures that don't have the necessary strength or teeth to kill them in a single blow. And Kaspar saw the trees being covered in snow, the leaves turning to ice; he sat quietly, with a certain rapacious goodwill, enjoying the frost caressing his head, when a hand swept that dream off his forehead.

The hand belonged to a gentleman who was looking at Kaspar with watchful keenness as he began to speak:

"My good sir," he said, "I know I am disturbing you, you were obviously immersed in something pleasant, at least, I hope you were; as you can see, I am trying to be civil. I've just returned from a place in need of a tutor: the building, seen from the outside, seemed suitable to me—sooty, bleak, run-down—and within there were stairs, hallways, lead-white and carmine walls, and even glass-vaulted galleries. I had not thought, as I entered confidently, who the young people to be placed in my care—whether as their tutor, domestic, or nanny—might be. In the hallways some boys were blue in the face from the gusts of cold air but they didn't seem to care, they stared ahead to where other boys were sitting, and it seemed that they might be staring into the bones of their own features, finding deeply etched circles under their eyes, and who knows, perhaps California, the canyons, or avenues of trees lined up and squared as in an accountant's ledger. 'Who are they?' I asked. 'They're melancholics, sir, can't you see?'

"I went up to the second floor: six windows to one side of the door, six to the other, and all one saw out those windows was the intransigent reality of a landscape that nothing could alleviate—a courtyard, a playing field, and a wall. Have you ever visited that kind of place? Doesn't it make you feel weary even before you begin? To walk around places you have no wish to see, looking at objects and people of no interest, only to be dismayed when other rooms are thrown open? That was how I felt when a door opened.

"Are you looking at me? Those boys, too, said that my eyes seem steeped in brine. I am by nature a domestic—my name is Lampe. I lived for many years on two floors of a comfortable house, with a widower. All of a sudden he bid me farewell, forever. I don't know where he might be now. He often searched for images of homes that take in elderly people; he dwelled on the pictures of reading rooms, where one or two people with glasses and mild expressions look at a light falling with no rays over the green leather tops of ebony desks.

"And now I often come to this garden, which has become my classroom. I watch the life of birds and other animals; I seldom go home without having slipped some gift of nature carefully into my pocket: some soggy moss, a stone, the anomalous part of a plant, or drops of resin gleaming on a strip of bark. I see myself spectrally in trees. I understand the distaste you feel in my company. I am familiar with the impatience we feel when forced to suspend the enchantment of solitude …"

"Would you like," Kaspar proposed out of politeness, "to come to my place one day?"

"No," Lampe replied. "I don't pay visits: naturally, sir, I allowed myself to accept your card. I have more than one, and those names seem born of the imagination, like encounters that never took place: Otto Wegener, Verena Küpferli. Encounters that took place, if you like, but the words (premeditated as they are) jolt me: imagine, sir, a rather old gentleman offering a tribute to his defective memories, as he stares at those yellowing bits of paper. Perhaps he utters some of the names out loud, reads the names of the streets, he may even have entered number 55 on some street once … perhaps he looked at its ruins … And he doesn't have the strength to take a match and allow those bits of paper to burn, as he holds them between his fingers."

* * *

KASPAR: That same evening I invited Lampe to come with us to the pavilion.

KATRIN: At that time I slept on a small bed in a corner of the room, a very narrow bed, and I would watch my companion, the widower Kaspar, who shared his existence with me. At times, toward evening, the monotony and tedium became almost unbearable, but I was pliant and yielded to what I supposed must be the order of the universe. It was as though smoke had curled his hair, and—thanks to the brutal simplicity that my mute companion was able to spread all around him—even someone who lived in dread of imminent catastrophe stopped thinking about it altogether. Kaspar opened the windows to let cold air into the rooms and when it snowed, the wind blew all the snow it had stripped off the trees at us, and both of us, sitting on the bed, waited for winter to continue.

KATRIN: At one time, a certain water trough was very dear to me. Sitting on its stone rim, I'd spend long hours reading, and now and then passersby would talk to me. They'd throw their caps to the ground and touch the chilly water, and they seemed to have a lot of time at their disposal. Maybe they, too, contemplated that steel faucet, so austere and simple, or the little mold bubbles on the surface of the water. From the farthest field I could hear the cowbells—then they would go away, and I liked that everyone had a destination. A water trough was an intermediate place, made of gray stone, and an unshakable tendency toward concrete things drew me to that cool sheltered place. Herders also came by. The horses' tender wet nostrils plunged into the water. And the passersby, tall, solid, and stockily built, whose shoes were sometimes larger than their feet and wider, whose eyebrows were singed by willpower, and their gaze clouded behind stubborn orbs—it seemed to me that they did not own themselves: they were, rather, absent people, who took their body out of its lair simply to let themselves pass from one extreme to another. When they trotted away on horses, quickly, they seemed happy to be going so far away already.

KATRIN: Only five minutes have gone by since I saw a crow against the trees and sky—after a brief exalted flight it walked maimed and quickly toward me. You must have seen eagles walk in aviaries, their stride a majestic agony, their eyes burnished with hate offering a farewell. I did not feel, at that moment, the puritanical inclination to turn an innocuous vision into a fairy tale, but looking at that crow, there was in its way of lingering, of keeping still, a kind of obstinate waiting, as if it were following a thought, an almost spiritual thought, as if she were about to say something to me, perhaps to tell me to think about water—or to follow her, I didn't know. I tried to understand, looking into her eyes, but the crow's eyes were turned elsewhere, after having met my gaze with two minuscule swatches of velvet. I tried to touch her, but the crow withdrew, without flying, she walked away, calmly. Unwittingly, I ran after that leaden awkward mass advancing carefully toward the cliff. There, limestone humps drop down to the water, solemnly, lethargically. At that sundown hour the rocks are a sickly green, they enter the water with marshy reflections. It was as though the crow could smell the long-lost ships, she stared at the shadows and the first stars, without understanding how distant they were. Meanwhile the feathered mantle was opening, the splits of the wings started to bend. Inadvertently I grazed her elbow, she had elbows like mine, and at the same height. She smiled faintly, as though she felt a kind of obscure and cautious glee in seeing that I was like her, that she had mimicked my features.

"You must know, Katrin," said the crow, "that I yearned for peace, I had been flying all around here for years, outside your window, and so as not to be seen, I clung to the wall and watched you; I could only see half of you. I saw a torso and long hair move through the room. For a long time I thought you didn't have any feet, I grew fond of you, of the torso, of that maimed thing. And that unfortunate child kept me company. I spoke to her, I traveled with you, but close to the ground so she couldn't hear. You hardly slept, you asked for the bed to be placed in front of the window, so that you might see the snow and the drifts. And now I would like to ask you a question: you were sometimes truly lighthearted, you laughed with a sweet open laugh. Who with? There was no one in the room with you. I thought of the intolerant gaiety of children, and looked at your teeth laughing at the walls. And I wished that you would talk to me, to that thing flying on the other side of the wall."

KATRIN: Yesterday she was down there by the end of the wall, standing stiff, a black sash at the waist and a positive look in her eyes. Small irises. Is she contemplating? Our eyes meet.

I lowered my gaze heavily. The cracks in the walls rustled, she was leaving: a faint smell of game and face powder lingered in the room. I opened the window, I saw her in the garden resting her feet on my trestles which had patiently been constructed by Lampe and painted blue. "You thief, thief," I repeated.

But she moved away more and more, I saw her once more crouching in the branches of a tree, she was torpid, elegant, a white ruff around her throat.

THE CROW: You can call me a thief if you like, a thief of ceremonies: by the time the echo of my phonic furor calls out the names of the people who are about to arrive—I met one of them in Amsterdam, more than once I perched on the shoulders of one of his statues, till he began to think that I was part of a still life: you'll find it strange, my dear, but more than once I saw his shadow pass by here—I'll be far away.

Here they are:

* * *

Beeklam
Victor

* * *

And soon after, cinched correctly in capes they wear only when traveling:

* * *

Magdalena
Rosalind

KATRIN: A crystal finger knocks on the door ... It is Lampe.

* * *

A while later, Lampe's solemn shaved features appeared at the door, wearing the finest of his black suits, he seems to have slipped into the room and through life like a seal through water. But he was not sociable like seals and he had nothing else in common with them. No decision or intention seemed to come with him, perhaps only the starched shirt reminded him of how one can remain standing and uncreased before the apathetic smiles of one's destiny.

* * *

KATRIN: What do you want? [she said turning her slow gaze, with something in her eyes that was a fraction less than a smile]

LAMPE: Night is falling much faster than the twilight might have led one to suppose.

KATRIN: So you'll feel you've waited less, they'll be here soon.

LAMPE: I thought I heard their names.

KATRIN: Those names were in fact called out.

LAMPE: I also take pleasure in waiting interminably—and as you can see, my dear, I am leaving right away, I know that you are not a tireless listener ...

KATRIN: Was there something you wanted to tell me today?

LAMPE: I like to let go of things that are close to me so as to run backward, toward times that are by now extinguished.

KATRIN: Or hollow.

LAMPE: I know I've mentioned this to you before. When I entered the pavilion for the first time and presented my references, I began by saying, "I like to let go of things that are close to me." I had walked a long way to reach this place, who knows if Beeklam and Victor will manage to get here, they are so old, it might be their last journey, as mine will be, too.

KATRIN: Last voyages are nearly always smooth.

LAMPE: That day the mud was full of cracks, it felt as though I had sand between my teeth as I spoke, I thought: the young lady has not understood. And I was wrong. The young lady may also be looking back, she had no need to look at me, she had already turned away from me. If there are words that the young lady understands, they would have to be rooted in sand and trampled by camels. Are you expecting anyone else, mademoiselle? I asked her, since she was holding black binoculars in her hand. I immediately accepted the room I was offered, as a large low fan with yellow blades blew frost over my ears. Hoping to quickly conclude the matter of my references, it was with ease that I proceeded to inform her of the education I had received, and again I repeated: "I was reared to respect and venerate all adults and particularly the elderly. I was taught that it was my duty to lend a hand wherever necessary. The importance of listening to, and immediately carrying out, the wishes and commands of parents and domestic personnel had been instilled in me. I feel as though I am living among busboys and barbers."

KATRIN [exiting the corridor]: There is, in helping others, a vague homicidal passion hard to contain in less bloody impulses.

LAMPE: I pretended not to hear, she had by now left me alone in a room I'd like to call a parlor, and I went on: "And that world of male societies, of camaraderie, which, as you know is not founded on the individuality of the partners, but perhaps on a memory of long gone corporations, did not inspire affection in me. On the contrary, it drilled into me a tacit acceptance of hatred. But when I realized I needed silence and friendship, I looked for a mute companion. And that's how I started canvassing houses in search of domestic work. I thought that this companion must have a house, an establishment and a spiritual well-being of his own, a fountain pen, a kitchen, curtains and whole sets of small things that creak inside cabinetry. Peacefully, the mute companion sits on a bench, almost as though there might be an obscure pleasure in taming oneself." Then I fell silent.

On a warm and rank summer night, Beeklam and Victor, accompanied by the echo of their names, without either rushing or hesitating, approached the light of a large house. The streetlamp gave it an appearance of slumbering gold. They found their feet resting on the tiles of a square barren drawing room. It is perhaps needless to say that they felt they had entered a dream, or a catastrophe, or simply a new life.

Capes slide off shoulders and Lampe takes them away. In the entrance stands a gloomy wardrobe. The wind has subsided, a shy silence everywhere, so empty and weak that a storm might have burst in at any moment. In a hollow of the corridor shivering men can be seen who have a few memories in common, but above all share a vocation for remembering: something brutal and celestial, related at one time to innocence and the powers unleashed by the earth. They seem kind, appealing, even capable of sorrow; fusty and remote, they shake hands, embrace; it is a farewell rather than a greeting.

In that waiting room, whose peace was seldom disturbed by tradesmen, Beeklam and Victor wait, they seem content to remain by the threshold, before a fan with thick blades. Lampe tries to point to a room, with the index finger of a tax collector tired of preambles. He had impatiently awaited their arrival, without sleeping, and his morose lids, no longer holding up, refused another vigil: he wished that the encounter had already taken place, and his wish was fulfilled.

"Sit," Katrin said without affectation or courtesy. Beeklam took off his glasses and let some character transpire in his eyes, a vacuous expression. Wherever he went, around the rooms or in the garden, he seemed to be only partially there, giving off a sense of unease; he addressed others as if he were a confessor, spoke very softly, hardly a murmur, with a sibilating sound that often spells spite. If he said that it was a magnificent morning, his tone seemed to suggest that it was deplorable that the morning should be magnificent. Victor watched him and was puzzled, in the basements Beeklam was, somehow, more at ease, content in the dark, his breath robbing the statues of air almost gleefully. And receiving a sadness that conjured joys of the past, the dungeon had lost its moldy desperation. Year after year, Beeklam had precisely described the places and stones to which he felt bound, to which he "owed" a return, he spoke of the last rays of sunset touching the reefs, as if truly, next to the sewers and water pipes, his horizon might blend with the sky. Whereas now, before that much praised landscape, his words were stifled, his eyes traveled no further than a quarter inch.

Time went by. It had a dull effect on Katrin. Plants flowered and wilted; when color was drained from things and the nights grew longer and passed unheeded, Katrin impatiently awaited the clay and diamond hues that precede the dawn. She considered everything ephemeral as her property, though her days meandered elsewhere, in a land with no rules, in which perfection has no heirs.

In his shelter beneath a dark green roof, by the cottage gate, a mastiff dozed. In that cottage, a few miles from the pavilion, Katrin and Gertrud, a rich farmer from Westphalia, were talking. It wasn't the first time that Katrin had left; she disappeared for whole days, would find shelter with one lady or another who had chosen that landscape, that solitude of rugged stones, to end their existence, or to continue it, rather, as forgotten women, or so they told Katrin, "as if we had suddenly been plummeted into another nature where the breath is foreign and involuntary." "I have known suffering," Gertrud said, but did not give off that light that the fleeting wonders of grief can bring, she spoke of it as though reading from an account book; every one of her dead had brought her gifts of money and revenues. She had narrow lips, Gertrud, a thin nose, and was as tall as the armoires in her house. Beneath prominent jaws, a gray crepe collar flecked with violet hid her neck. The eyes were flat as Alpine lakes that sweetly reflect celestial iniquities. Katrin thought that that woman had carried the furniture on her shoulders all the way from Germany, with the gifts from her dead in the palms of her hands.

"In the evening," Gertrud said, "before I left my country, I would take a walk with my stick, the fields were overrun with weeds, and sometimes I would encounter single trees by the side of the road underneath which farmers in times of peace would surely have found shade and rest. The war had given that landscape a heroic and melancholy tinge, though without destroying its grace; the opulent flowering was heady and appeared to be even more radiant. It's easy, my dear, I thought then, to struggle in a landscape such as this one, rather than in a cold and desolate wintry setting. There even a simple soul feels that her life takes on a profound assurance and that her death is not an end. I have not forgotten the war, Katrin, nor Westphalia."

KATRIN: My friend Eleanor was born into a distinguished family from Massachusetts. The father, a Puritan, was a lawyer who looked on every mental digression with suspicion. Theatricality and elaborate displays of passions could never inebriate him. He had that incorruptible, willful coldness that strives only for precision, but beyond that quality all else remained undefined. He bore an ancient English name and saw to it that his family lived according to principles handed down by his forebears. They had emigrated in 1634, and so considered themselves the true Americans. Ever since then, none of the forebears had stopped having disputes with the law. Justice and fanaticism still shone in the father's yellow eyes, his hands — a trellis of bones — often stroked, in the course of the day, a judge's gown and wig, the round cap of an inkwell, and sticks of sealing wax. Sometimes it seemed that his imposing presence unsettled his daughter, but it wasn't so: Eleanor had some affection for her father, though piety was not in her nature. But it was with fervor that they debated late into the night, before the fire, unresolved cases of homicide. And in Massachusetts there were no lack of homicides. Eleanor sometimes encountered, on her way back from school, men with dark sacks on their shoulders, behind the mowed hedges. But she had learned to be afraid of nothing and never hurried home. Instead, it was with melancholy and painful joy that she viewed assassins in court: they had to atone. She possessed, in fact, a vision of legality as a whole as well as the composure to never rail against the most hideous of deeds. Nothing remarkable happened to her till she turned twenty-five. During a three-week stay in England she met a forty-seven-year-old Protestant pastor, and a deep understanding stirred between them. The pastor already had a wife and daughters, so love came to Eleanor wearing the stern face of renunciation.

KATRIN: "Wearing the stern face of renunciation"—those promising words pushed me to go out. It was late spring, the nightingales joyfully trill their long-repressed ecstasies. I walk skirting the walls; austere triumphant women glide along the pavement. I carried a dark bag on my shoulder. A lacemaker undid her embroidery and her slim fingers were made of ice. I looked at the windows, the lit interiors, yellowing hair bending toward ashes in a fireplace, playing with embers with a little shovel, while soot-covered girls climb into chimney flues, they climb higher and higher, and up on the roofs they count the stars, that drifting gold.

KATRIN: She was very firm when she said goodbye. With the self-satisfied grace of one who considers that something has come to an end, she held out her hand: there was in her a warrior's vigor, tempered by a mellow weariness. The light, meanwhile, after having crossed the hallway windows (at the Hotel de Russie) fell onto details of the sumptuous tapestries on the walls, almost malignantly; there are moments, it's true, when light seems to travel against the wind. Eleanor propelled me toward the exit, long goodbyes are draining. Behind us, the doorman in a visor cap and little stars consulted a register and with his little fingers pushed the cuffs up into his sleeves. How would he take leave of a friend?

The hotel guests, seated in large armchairs, finish their cigars with leisurely deliberation. The newspapers hung from rods, overly polished teapots sat on silver trays, and floral decorations were lavishly distributed.

As for Eleanor, who viewed assassins in court with wistful joy, I never saw her again.

KATRIN: Eleanor has dwelled in my memory for the past few hours; on the path that leads me toward the dunes, the rocks seem dressed in her suits: the color's the same, ashen.

* * *

Before Katrin's eyes lay the earth where she was perhaps born and where she lived, a gigantic fatal hotel for unaccompanied children who chewed on boredom, and maybe the land of her childhood was really down there, steeped in shadow where the cliffs end, where the water starts to move, shielded from the oppression of celestial light.

* * *

In the evening, Katrin returned to the pavilion. She saw Kaspar sitting in the veranda. That night the moonlight was as solid as marble and took a seat at the table, adhering to the curve of the high backrest. Kaspar caressed that beloved frozen shadow and began to eat. He slowly helped himself to some vegetables. Every single thing the nocturnal light touched seemed endowed with a fierce blissful light. The zucchini darkened on porcelain plates. Kaspar sat on until that lunar effusion headed elsewhere.

VICTOR: You are happy here, Lampe, are you not?

LAMPE: One says goodbye to everything here; in places like these it's as if all that is yet to happen were already in the past. The Bernese Oberland beats at my temples. Little could now distract me from my conversation with those soldiers, those mercenaries who were my forebears. Beneath the elms, their eyes as if hammered in place by blacksmiths, still nurturing a secret rage—and I am in doubt. In some part of creation I exist in every way like them, and sometimes I cannot distinguish between the rage that possesses me and the peace I have inflicted on myself.

LAMPE: I'll have to sound the gong soon.

VICTOR: As in old times. Impeccably punctual. When I entered Beeklam's house for the first time—he was still a child—I thought: an orphan and already a collector. Right then a crate almost nine feet high entered. The crate immediately went downstairs and I went upstairs, to the second floor. My room faced a blind alley. I planted a fruit tree. Who knows whether it grew.

LAMPE: I must leave you, Katrin is punctual.

VICTOR: Ever since then we have always lived together, we have gone from fervent to lukewarm, and finally to something resembling a cautious balance. And, as in fairy tales, we have come back up from the basements, laden with the years, tranquil, unwearied, almost not alive.

LAMPE: With your father, Mr. Reginald, I got along well. He was quiet, often he would tell me that he would have liked to live with a man who talked all the time. He would have sat at his feet and would've had to do nothing other than be attentive and listen, eyes wide open. I felt, as the years passed, that he was more and more disposed to seek the company of anyone except me. And in the end I withdrew, I let that little bit of joy, of elegance, the ardor that galvanizes the gaze and transfigures the face, gradually fade. Of Thelma, the ephemeral wife, there is no longer even a trace, a photograph, or an embroidery. He got rid of it all and when he told me he was a widower, he seemed apologetic.

VICTOR: "I am certain that only egoism brings peace," Thelma told me one day, as she ran her fingers over the silver embroidery hemming her cape, "and sometimes those who repent die of sheer desperation. You, Victor," she continued, "will certainly think I am a ridiculous creature, like so many others in this world; pompous, demented, headed for putrefaction. You've seen that I am very weak. Tell me, sir, what do you think of life? I know how to listen, I am keen to once again grasp the visible signs—the physical presence of a stranger." Then she said, "What is the difference, after all, between a scornful laugh and a grimace of fear? It may seem strange to you, but I

74

am still full of curiosity with respect to life; though I've always been somewhat reluctant to approach what I was attracted to."

While she spoke, I looked at her face, there was something wild and at the same time ascetic about her, and if she glanced at me furtively I caught in her eyes the desire to penetrate into the mind of another so as to find there the same distaste for life that tormented her.

LAMPE: Reginald is timid, too. He has always been calm and serene, almost as though he were gliding, without the help of feathers, or wings: all that sustained him was the simple play of contrary forces between Eternity and Time, that's how he liked to speak. And one day he ran away from home. He had just turned seventy. Just as he's about to disappear, he displays, on turning around, the liveliness of a young man, with a grace made both of majesty and that amiable freedom sometimes found in saints and the elderly—smiling, he blows me a kiss from the tips of his fingers, with the same hand he would use to bless me. He never came back.

BEEKLAM: I know where he is.

I had been walking for many hours, obeying a wooden arrow pointing to a mountain inn. I had searched for my father in vain, as you know I had left him very early on. It is odd how suddenly the urge comes over us to find a certain person who has disappeared, and we are naive enough to think that lost things become so small, idle, and wayward that we might suddenly find them again on the ground. We bend down, pick them up, and put them in our pocket. And it is with that sentiment that I started to look for Reginald. I knew that he was too old to be a guest among the living, till I reached a garden on top of a mountain. Amid geometric flower beds bands of human beings, who barely moved, descended stone steps toward a rectangle of stale water. They progressed tentatively, shaking their head: they were old men and women, some seemed to be agreeing, others disagreeing with something. Witnessing those ancient and stubborn itinerants affirming and denying, those frail gestures, I thought: "One cannot do otherwise." And I found myself before a wooden hut. Behind clouded glass, at the end of a small room, I encountered the lost happy glance of a man who wore the same clothes as my father—threadbare and dank. I approached cautiously. Without shifting his gaze, the man whispered haltingly: "My son." I was astounded, and said in a fit of rage, "Why didn't you call me?" All the other gentlemen, seated or leaning against the glass of a veranda over-looking a snowy mountain, smiled imperceptibly. "It's his son," they murmured, and touched an imaginary son of their own with lukewarm fingers. Such was everyone's astonishment, and the enchanted surprise of seeing a stranger in their midst, that they surrounded me as though pulled by threads.

"Why, Father? Why did you pretend to be dead, when I was looking for you?"

"I'm sorry, I'm sorry," he replied. "I'll never do it again."

"What is going on here?" a man in uniform shouted at that moment, leaping onto a marble table. "Can't you see that they are drunk, truly drunk, sir? Are you here to identify someone? Go away." He pushed me out the door. It was a livid winter day.

LAMPE: I had just sounded the gong. Katrin sat reluctantly, she is not speaking. Only an exaggerated impulse could have induced Beeklam to confide in her. And I saw Beeklam's words land on her face, and fall, pecking at the fruit gathered onto the tray, and leaving with me as I cleared the table.

KATRIN: Rosalind and Magdalena arrived one winter evening and felt—or so they said, if I remember correctly—a sense of solitude and fear, as if in some part of the dark cliffs the light of one lamp was still lit by an empty eternity, as it spread its sickly doleful flame; but it was beautiful and in a way brought some serenity. It illuminated the night, the walls of the house, and it seemed, they said, to bypass those who were inside it. "Katrin, Katrin," they spoke my name with a pitiful screech from lips belonging to those who can only love with their soul but don't want embraces and fear kisses as though they might mutilate. "Katrin," they called my name again, touching my shoulder with a humble and heavy symmetrical gesture. The small joys of childhood had left a lovely clear light in their eyes and when they lowered their lids, I realized that they were chipped. They looked like two statues to me.

MAGDALENA: From the north windows of our house in Amsterdam we could see a five-story gray building, spare and stingy. It obscured the sun and the polished light that appears as night turns into dawn. We never saw any lights in those rooms across from us. Rosalind and I went to live in that house ever since, on a distant school day, a soft warmth had joined our childish existences and our friendship had seemed imbued with that deaf delight of the conviction that one has found the right person.

ROSALIND: In those years, dear Mademoiselle Katrin, we did not love human beings, whether children or adults. All the same, naturally, we helped others, and Magdalena, with her distinguished well-groomed face, and stock of good clothes, fulfilled all obligations having to do with doing good, with great composure. Doing good, Magdalena would say, is something soulless, between a ritual and a compass.

BEEKLAM: I am sitting on a bench in the garden. I don't know what I am waiting for. Two geese provide an illusion of movement, their feet are about to walk away, they have, almost, a marching attitude—and on seeing that suppressed impulse, a goose swallowing her dreams, I am surprised suddenly by the lack of faces during my long hours of wakefulness.

KATRIN: At that time the garden endured an invasion of snails. Lazily they devastated the verbena with their invisible shears. Every night, large cabbage leaves covered with beer drops were scattered over the flower beds, and at dawn, each one, like a trap, was transformed into a green drawing room teeming with intoxicated snails.

The persons evoked herein are standing before the sundial, beside the reflecting pools, witnessing midday land on them. A wide-brimmed hat covers Magdalena's and Rosalind's brows. From beneath chipped lids, placid eyes gaze at Time. Katrin sweeps away the footprints, the sundial goes on marking time, with its small angular shadow, black and slithery on the tepid stone.

THE END

EPILOGUE

KATRIN: Distractedly, I came to a blind alley. In the middle of it was an apple tree so laden with fruit it rested on crutches, almost as though such opulence could only result in infirmity. The placid earth of the pavement invited me to linger a while longer. Metallic nets swayed from the house and solid shadows moved, as though they felt, half an hour away, the ineffable winds of destiny. An obese boy went by whistling. His features were smooth and he wore a black suit with white stripes. His puffy temples shone and his hair was brushed back. From a waistcoat the alarm on a pocket watch trilled. The year before three people had hung themselves in that house: a Swiss traveling salesman, a bicycle-riding evolutionist, and a student of botany, said the boy. And he pointed to a room. "Up there," he said. "And I wouldn't be surprised if one or another of them came toward me. But since they haven't already done so, I couldn't care less. Are you waiting for someone? I know that you often come here. I am a bit of a spy, you see, usually I am able to recognize, even years later, people I've seen only once. I take possession of the faces of people passing by, as others might look at plants. But I don't look at plants. Nature, so often celebrated, does not enchant me, I am completely indifferent to it. I put the crutches here, supporting this tree, it enchanted me. If there weren't exceptions, why look at all that surrounds us?

"Whereas people's faces give me the impression that they could fit in the large palm of my hand, between my fat disgusting fingers. For me, to turn my eyes onto their faces—since it looks as though I'll be a giant, at my age one keeps growing a lot more—yes, for me," he said, "it is like erasing time because all those faces etched in my memory become fixed, and so my relationship to the world in movement is somewhat altered; and that is how I erase time—blowing once on the palm of my hand I extinguish the awful flow of hours. Don't you find it flows too quickly? That it sweeps us away too soon, only certain trees are centuries old, shouldn't there be an extra century of existence? Because then, even if the hours were to be filled to bursting, it wouldn't matter, there would still be that extra century we wished for at our disposal. I am very nearly disgusted at how soon this life ends. Look at me, I am a child, but tomorrow I'll already be fully exposed to the searchlights of old age, of decrepitude. And I'm not even through high school yet. I am still at that ungrateful age when one is ugly and flabby, though I am almost grateful for this state of transient puffiness, it makes me think there will be that other phase, too, of thinness. Doesn't it bother you that we live so briefly? I think it does. It seems that time—though you aren't much older than me—has gnawed at your cheeks a little, but has left your girlish features intact. And now I must leave you, I must invent a farewell I can place in my souvenirs. Tell me, should I perhaps work for some organization, for the police, given my memory for physiognomies? Unfortunately I have no incentive to put this memory to good use."

The high-school student nodded goodbye, pointing to the sunset as the place he was probably headed to, and disappeared. Katrin heard steps on the cobblestones of the blind alley, and with the eyes of a silent sentinel watched the windows. They were dull, like a pillow made yellow by a head that had rested on it far too long; the last gestures of those who had lived in those rooms seemed pasted on the glass panes, stiff heavy shadows fell to pieces. In there, she thought, something was about to happen. Someone, as though death were a prolonged whimsy, pushed her away, with a rough and melancholic gesture. Could it be the three who'd hung themselves returning? Katrin thought about the student of botany, and the Swiss traveling salesman unfastening the rope. There was a blaze of fire on his face and the clothes barely fluttered in the night breeze. Katrin moved on, slowly; she was in no rush to arrive anywhere. In the finest hour of the night, freshness turned to squalor.